WONDER WOMAN™

BOOK OF THE FILM

WONDER WOMAN™

BOOK OF THE FILM

ADAPTED BY STEVE KORTÉ

Wonder Woman created by
William Moulton Marston

centum

Wonder Woman: Book of the Film
A CENTUM BOOK 978-1-911460-36-7
Published in Great Britain by Centum Books Ltd
This edition published 2017

1 3 5 7 9 10 8 6 4 2

Centum Books Ltd, 20 Devon Square, Newton Abbot, Devon, TQ12 2HR
books@centumbooksltd.co.uk

CENTUM BOOKS Limited Reg. No. 07641486
A CIP catalogue record for this book is available from the British Library
Printed inUK

MIX
Paper from
responsible sources
FSC® C018072

WONDER WOMAN™

BOOK OF THE FILM

I t was shortly after six o'clock in the morning as the sun rose in Paris, France. The Louvre Museum, rose-colored with the dawn, was several hours away from opening. Museum guards paced slowly through the empty galleries, occasionally glancing at the world-famous paintings and sculptures they were hired to protect. In a remote wing of the museum, down a long and dark hallway, one light was shining.

The light came from the office of Diana Prince, a curator for the museum and one of the world's leading experts in ancient art. Her office was filled with Greek antiquities and ancient weapons. This morning, Diana sat at her desk, lost in thought.

Diana was a young woman, tall and with an athletic build. Her long, black hair was pulled back in a ponytail. Even though she had been working in her office all night long, she didn't appear to be tired. Instead, she stared at an ornate globe of the world that stood at the far edge of her desk.

"I wanted to protect the world," she said quietly to herself. "To honor my people and the mission they were given. To end war and bring peace to mankind."

She wondered what her coworkers at the museum would say if she told them that Diana Prince was not her real name. A smile spread across her face, as she thought about telling them, "My real name is Diana, and I am an Amazon princess from the island of Themyscira."

She laughed lightly, picturing the shocked looks on their faces as she divulged one more secret: "By the way, you probably know me best as Wonder Woman. I left my home and my people—the Amazons—years ago to come to your world. My mission was to end a dangerous threat that could have destroyed the entire human race."

Diana's mind traveled back to that day, many years ago, when she had joined the human world to fight evildoers and spread a message of peace. She had eagerly taken on her new role as protector of mankind. Soon she became known as the mighty hero Wonder Woman.

Diana's smile faded as she reached for a small wooden crate that had been delivered to her office the night before. A label on the box identified the sender: Wayne Enterprises.

Diana was one of the few people in the world who knew that Bruce Wayne, the owner of Wayne Enterprises, was secretly the crime-fighting hero known as Batman. Why had Bruce sent her a package now?

Diana pried the nails loose from the top of the crate and lifted the lid. She gasped as she removed a brown-tinged photograph from the box. It was a daguerreotype, an antique photo from 1918. Diana instantly recognized the image, and the events that led to its existence came rushing to her mind. She was standing in the middle of the photo, wearing her Amazonian armor. She had a shield at her side, and she wore a grim but determined look on her face. Four men stood next to her, each carrying a rifle. The battle-scarred buildings of a village in Belgium could be seen behind them. In the background of the photo, there were soldiers wearing British uniforms from World War I.

Diana reached into the box and removed an unsigned note.

"I found the original photo. Maybe one day you'll tell me your story," it said.

Diana stared at the photo. *My story*, she thought. *I knew so little then. The world was not as simple as I thought. And mankind was another story altogether.*

She stared at the faces of the men in the photo.

"But, thanks to *them*," she said, "I will never be the same."

Diana's mind drifted back to a time many years before World War I and to a place far away from Belgium. She smiled as she remembered an island in the middle of the ocean. It seemed so long ago. . . .

ONE

C *LANG!*
      The sound of swords crashing filled the air. It was a beautiful, sunny day, and dozens of women were battling each other on a grassy field near the ocean shore. The women were all strong, athletic, and wore suits of armor. Most of them were carrying weapons. Some held swords in their hands, while others used knives or spears. One armored woman rode atop a horse and lassoed another woman with a rope.

They were the Amazons, a legendary race of

warrior women who lived far from the rest of the world on their secret island of Themyscira. Every day, they traveled to this field to train for a battle they hoped would never come.

Two women, both in peak physical condition, faced each other in the middle of the field. Their names were Artemis and Eliana, and they both clasped swords in their hands. Another woman, taller and wearing a richly decorated metal helmet, stood next to them. She was General Antiope, one of the bravest and strongest of the Amazons. She watched closely as Artemis savagely swung her sword and knocked Eliana to the ground. A fierce smile of triumph filled Artemis's face.

"Yes, the blow was strong, but Eliana's footwork betrayed her," said Antiope. "A battle is like a river crossing. Every step must find a safe spot."

At the edge of the field, an eight-year-old girl was watching the action with fascination. When Artemis swung her sword, the girl lifted her tiny hands and mimicked her movements with an imaginary sword. Her name was Diana, and more than anything in the world, she longed to join the Amazons in their training. Suddenly, a voice came from behind her.

"Diana! Diana, I *see* you!"

Diana froze at the edge of the field for a second, and then she began to run. The voice belonged to Mnemosyne, her tutor. Diana was supposed to be studying today.

"Diana, come back!" called Mnemosyne.

Diana bolted across the field, darting past the battling Amazons. She ran straight to the crowded marketplace near the center of Themyscira.

One Amazon after another smiled at Diana as she zoomed past.

"Hello, Diana," said one.

"Good morning, Princess Diana," said another.

Diana was the only child on Themyscira, and the Amazons had grown accustomed to seeing her run through the city, racing to elude her tutor.

Even an Amazon guard, her arms outstretched to capture the running child, was no obstacle for Diana. She easily slid between the guard's legs and ran up a set of narrow stone steps.

The stairs led to a steep cliff, and Diana barely paused before she leaped off the edge. She soared through the air for a few seconds, but realized that she had jumped way farther than she intended. She was falling. As her descent picked up speed, a look of panic filled her face. She was about to crash to the ground.

Suddenly, a hand shot out and grabbed her wrist. Diana looked around and saw the disapproving face of her mother, Queen Hippolyta, who was the leader of the Amazons. A silver crown glinted atop the queen's head, and her long blond hair stirred in the wind as she glared at her daughter.

"Hello, Mother," Diana said sweetly. "How are you today?"

Hippolyta shook her head sadly and asked, "How many times, Diana?"

"I haven't actually counted," admitted Diana. "Quite a few?"

Hippolyta grasped Diana's wrist tighter and started pulling her away.

"Let's get you back to school before another tutor quits," said Hippolyta.

Diana protested, "But Mother . . . don't you think it's time to start my training?"

"Training? You *are* training," said Hippolyta.

The queen paused and crouched down in front of her daughter.

"Your mind is your most powerful weapon. All battles begin here . . . ," she said, pointing her finger at Diana's head.

". . . before they end here," she concluded, gesturing to the world around them.

Just then, General Antiope arrived, riding on a horse. She dismounted and bowed to the queen.

"General Antiope thinks I'm ready!" said Diana.

"*Does* she?" Hippolyta asked as she glanced at Antiope.

"I could begin showing her some things," offered Antiope. "She should at least be able to defend herself."

"From whom?" the queen asked.

"In the event of an invasion," replied Antiope.

"Isn't that why I have an army at my command, General?" asked Hippolyta icily.

"I pray a day will never come where she has to fight, but you, *the wisest of us all*, know that an Amazon cannot deny her inner nature."

"She's a child. The *only* child on the island," said Hippolyta. "Please, let her be so."

"But, Sister . . . ," began Antiope.

"But, Mother . . . ," protested Diana.

"There will be *no* training," Hippolyta declared, putting the conversation to an end.

TWO

Diana did not give up easily, though. That night, Hippolyta struggled to get her wide-awake daughter to close her eyes and go to sleep. Each time Hippolyta tucked Diana under the blankets on her bed, her daughter struggled loose.

"What if I promise to be careful?" pleaded Diana.

"It's time to sleep," Hippolyta said gently.

"What if I don't use a sword?"

"Fighting doesn't make you a hero," was the queen's weary response.

"Just a shield then. No sharp edges!"

"Diana, you are the most precious thing in this world to me," said Hippolyta. "So much so, I sculpted you from clay and begged Zeus to give you life."

Diana frowned and threw herself back against her pillow.

"You've *told* me that story," she pouted.

"Then I will tell you a *new* one," said Hippolyta. "One of our people, and my days of battle. So you will finally understand . . . why *war* is nothing to hope for!

"Long ago, when time was new, and all of history was a dream, the gods ruled the Earth," Hippolyta continued. "Zeus was the king among them. He created beings over which the gods would rule: beings born in his image, fair and good, strong and passionate. Zeus called his creation . . . man. And mankind was *good*.

"But one grew envious of Zeus's love for mankind . . . and sought to corrupt his creation."

The queen's face darkened. "This was Ares. The God of War.

"Ares poisoned men's hearts with jealousy and suspicion. He turned them against one another. And *war* ravaged the Earth. So the gods made us, the Amazons, to influence men's hearts with love and to restore peace to the world."

"What happened to Ares, Mother?" asked Diana.

"He and Zeus battled," Hippolyta replied. "Zeus used the last of his power to stop Ares, striking him with such a blow that the God of War was forced to retreat. But the battle killed Zeus. With his last dying breath, Zeus created this island to shield us from the outside world. Somewhere Ares could not find us. Here we can live peacefully in this paradise."

Diana's eyes began to close. As she drifted off to sleep, Hippolyta reached forward and lightly touched Diana's face.

"So you see, my daughter, you are safe. And it is nothing for you to concern yourself with." As she gazed down at her beautiful child, she only hoped she was right.

THREE

Four years later, Diana's dream finally came true. On that day she stood proudly with a sword in her hand and faced off against her aunt, General Antiope. A brief pang of guilt passed over Diana's face as she swung the heavy sword in the air. She had been forced to go behind her mother's back and beg Antiope to teach her basic combat skills. For several months, the two Amazons had been training in secret.

Antiope nodded approvingly as Diana thrust her sword forward. Then the older Amazon crashed her sword against Diana's, knocking the young girl off her feet. Diana tumbled to the ground.

"You're doubting yourself," observed Antiope.

"No, I'm not!" said Diana, as she quickly jumped to her feet and resumed her stance.

"Yes, you are," said Antiope. "But you *are* stronger than you believe."

"Diana!"

Diana and Antiope both froze. They knew who the voice belonged to, and they were trapped. They dropped their swords and turned to face Queen Hippolyta. She towered over them, sitting atop a giant white horse. She looked furious. Several Amazon guards stood behind her.

Diana spoke up quickly. "Mother . . . I'm fine . . . I was just . . ."

"Training," her mother said icily. "It seems that I am not the revered queen I should be. Disobeyed, betrayed, by my own sister!"

"Mother! It was *me*!" Diana said. "I asked General Antiope to—"

Hippolyta raised a hand and turned to the guards.

"Take Diana to the palace," she said.

As the crestfallen girl walked away, the queen glared at Antiope.

"You left me no choice, Hippolyta," said Antiope. "You neglect your duty if she cannot fight."

"You speak of a time that may never come," argued Hippolyta. "Ares may never return! He could have died of his wounds."

"*You think I don't wish that were true?*" Antiope raged. "But you feel it in your bones, just as I do. Ares is still alive. He is out there. And it's only a matter of time before he returns."

"But my daughter . . . ," Hippolyta said, as her voice trailed off.

Antiope put a hand on the queen's shoulder and said, "Nobody wants this less than I. I love her as you do. But this is the *only* way to *truly* protect her."

A look of determination came into Hippolyta's eyes, and she said, "If she must train, you will train her harder than every Amazon before her."

"Hippolyta—"

"Five times harder," demanded the queen. "*Ten* times harder. You will train Diana until she is *unconquerable*!"

FOUR

True to her word, Antiope and the other Amazons worked with the young princess until her feet were quick and her sword deftly carried. By the time she was grown, Diana could spar with the very best of the Amazon warriors and hold her ground. But still, she wanted more. She wanted to make her mother—her queen—proud.

One sunny day, Diana stood in the middle of the Amazon training field. A large crowd was gathered at the edge of the field. A proud smile filled Diana's face.

Today, she would prove to the other Amazons that she was their equal in strength and fighting ability.

Diana lifted a bow and arrow to her shoulder. She focused on the target far away at the other side of the field. Slowly she drew back the arrow and then let it fly.

"Bull's-eye!" cried out Menalippe, who was second-in-command.

For her next contest, Diana faced off against General Antiope herself. The two women lifted their shields and swords, preparing to battle. Soon, the harsh sounds of clashing swords filled the air. Diana fought superbly, returning each sword blow with a stronger one of her own. She smiled as she realized that she could easily hold her own against a more experienced opponent.

Suddenly, the crowd gasped. Artemis had stepped onto the field and was striding toward the two contestants. She carried her sword aloft, and she had a determined look on her face.

"Your combat skills have improved, Princess," Artemis called out defiantly. "But are you skilled enough to take on *two* opponents?"

Diana spun around in surprise, just as Artemis savagely swung her sword toward Diana.

Diana raised her shield and blocked the sword. She then kicked her leg forward with all her strength. Diana knocked Artemis off balance, causing her to topple onto the muddy field.

Diana felt movement behind her and turned to see Antiope swinging her sword. Diana deftly jumped aside to avoid the blow. *This was so easy,* she thought to herself.

"Come on, Diana. You're stronger than this," Antiope chided.

A look of grim determination filled Diana's face. She tightened her jaw and jumped forward to savagely attack her opponent. Diana thrust her sword toward Antiope over and over, forcing the older Amazon to raise her shield and step backward. A feeling of power filled Diana's body as it never had before. She felt that she could conquer *any* Amazon today.

With one savage blow, Diana knocked Antiope's sword from her hand. It fell to the ground with a loud *clang*. Diana smiled triumphantly over her fallen opponent, who had raised her hands in surrender.

She turned around to search for her mother in the crowd at the edge of the field. All the grueling years of training had been worth it. Hippolyta would now be forced to agree her daughter was a true warrior.

WHAM!

Out of nowhere, Antiope knocked Diana to the ground with a brutal blow. Diana groaned softly as she lay facedown in the mud.

At the edge of the field, sitting atop her white horse, Hippolyta looked on anxiously.

"Get up, Diana," she said under her breath.

Antiope spoke sternly to Diana, as the young Amazon shakily stood up.

"Never let your guard down!" said Antiope. "Your opponents will have *no* honor. They will strike you from *behind*! They will attack *without* provocation! Show me the Amazon you are! *Or was I wrong to put such faith in you?*"

Antiope expertly swung her sword at Diana, forcing her to stumble backward. Reflexively, Diana raised both arms to protect her face, slamming the silver bracelets on her wrists together.

BOOM!

The sound of an explosion filled the field. As the Amazons watched in astonishment, a bright blast of energy shot out of Diana's bracelets. The blast knocked Antiope to the ground.

Diana stumbled backward. She was ecstatic, scared, and confused. What had just happened? She looked over to her mother, hoping that Hippolyta could explain it. The queen was shaking her head sadly.

"Diana, what have you done?" asked Hippolyta.

The Amazons were staring at Diana in silence. Diana glanced down at Antiope. She saw that blood was streaming from a wound on Antiope's head.

"I'm so sorry . . . ," Diana said, as she stepped forward to offer assistance.

Antiope angrily held up her hand and said, "Stay back."

Diana slowly retreated. She glanced at her mother's forlorn face. Diana felt frightened, guilty, and rejected. She didn't know what she'd done, but she'd never felt this before—ashamed, outcast.

She began to run.

FIVE

Tears filled Diana's eyes as she stumbled through a forest at the edge of Themyscira. She ran faster and faster, not knowing or caring where she was going. Soon, she arrived at a grassy embankment on a cliff overlooking the ocean. She paused to wipe the tears from her eyes and glanced down at the bracelets on her wrists. With a shudder of fear, she clenched her eyes shut.

Lost in her thoughts, she tried to concentrate on the sound of the ocean waves crashing against the shore. It was a soothing sound. Just then, Diana heard another sound, an unfamiliar one. It sounded somewhat like a buzzing bee, but it was too loud. And it was getting closer. Diana opened her eyes and scanned the horizon. She was astonished to see a flying machine plummeting through the sky. Dark smoke was pouring from the rear of the plane.

Diana's sharp gaze focused on the front of the airplane. There was a man inside it, struggling to escape. Seconds later, the plane crashed into the ocean and sank beneath the surface.

Without hesitation, Diana jumped from the high cliff hundreds of feet above the ocean and dove into the clear blue waters. The plane was already sinking to the bottom of the ocean. Water was pouring in through a jagged hole in the glass cockpit, and the pilot was struggling to break free. As the plane continued to sink and the light faded, the pilot started to lose consciousness.

Suddenly, Diana appeared on top of the plane. She reached into the cockpit and grabbed the pilot. Bracing her feet against the falling airplane, she pulled the pilot free and carried him to the water's surface.

She easily hefted the unconscious man above the waves and swam to the shore. She then carried him to the warm, sandy beach and placed him gently on the ground.

Diana leaned over the pilot and stared at him in wonder. He was the first man she had ever seen. He appeared to be a few years older than Diana. He was tall, muscular, and broad shouldered. She closely studied his mouth, lips, sandy-blond hair, and the stubble of his beard. His clothes appeared to be some sort of uniform, and he wore a leather bag over his shoulders.

The man groaned softly, and then he opened his eyes, squinting in the bright sunlight. His first sight was Diana, leaning over him and studying his face.

"Wow," he said.

Diana quickly backed away, startled by his deep voice.

"You are a . . . man?" she asked.

"Yes, I mean . . . ," he began nervously. "Wait? Why do you ask? Do I not *look* like a man? Where am I?"

"You are on Themyscira," replied Diana.

"Thema . . . what? Say it again?"

"Who are you?" demanded Diana.

Before he could answer, the earsplitting sounds of scraping metal filled the air. A giant German battleship had crashed into the sharp protective reef that surrounded Themyscira. The damaged ship began to sink, but three smaller landing boats emerged from the battleship and started heading toward the beach.

"I'm one of the good guys," said the man. "And those are the *bad guys*!"

Diana looked confused, as she glanced from the man to the approaching boats.

"You know . . . *Germans*," said the man nervously.

"Germans?" asked Diana, as she watched the three boats with fascination.

"We gotta get out of here," said the man, as he jumped to his feet and grabbed Diana's hand to pull her away.

A commanding voice filled the air.

"Diana!" It was Queen Hippolyta.

The man looked up on the cliffs to see Hippolyta on horseback. She was riding toward the beach. The Queen's Guard rode behind her, dozens of armor-clad

Amazons, and they were all pointing arrows directly at the man who was holding Diana's hand.

"Step away from her! *Now!*" commanded Hippolyta.

The man turned to Diana and asked, "Where are their guns?"

Two dozen more Amazon guards on horseback arrived behind Hippolyta. They aimed their arrows at the German boats.

"Do they only have arrows?" asked the man. "We need guns. Because the Germans have guns. Lots and lots of—"

Before he could finish his sentence, a torrent of flaming arrows sailed from the top of the cliff and smashed into the three boats.

BLAM!

The soldiers in the boats raised their rifles and began firing at the Amazons. They continued to fire as they waded to the shore and moved onto the beach.

"Get down!" yelled the man next to Diana, as he pulled her out of the way. Bullets and arrows sailed above their heads. Together, they huddled behind a large rock at the edge of the beach.

More Amazons appeared at the top of the cliff.

They were led by the redheaded Amazon soldier Orana. She quickly surveyed the scene and shot a grappling arrow into the rock wall of a nearby cliff. Orana then swung down the line toward the beach, firing arrow after arrow at the approaching soldiers.

Diana watched with amazement as a German soldier lifted his rifle and pointed it directly at Orana. Time seemed to slow down as the gun exploded and a bullet emerged. Diana could actually see the bullet as it soared through the air. She watched with horror as it hit Orana, killing her instantly.

"No!" yelled Diana.

The soldiers continued to fire toward the top of the cliff, killing two more Amazons. The soldier who killed Orana lifted his rifle again and pointed it at General Antiope. He squinted into his rifle's scope.

WHUNK!

An arrow shot straight through the barrel of the rifle, killing the soldier.

The furious voice of General Antiope filled the air.

"Charge!" she called out, as a stampede of horse-women charged through a massive stone archway onto the beach. Riding at the front alongside Antiope was Menalippe, her second-in-command. The two Amazons swung their swords, knocking over German soldiers who were then trampled by the horses.

Diana jumped out from behind the rock and grabbed the sword and shield of a fallen Amazon. With a savage cry, Diana swung the sword and killed two more soldiers. The pilot grabbed one of the rifles and started shooting.

Suddenly, Hippolyta arrived on the beach. She urged her horse to go faster as she charged into the battle. Her sword whistled in the air as she cut down a dozen soldiers at once. Hippolyta joined Antiope and Menalippe, and together the three Amazon warriors fought side by side. They ruthlessly slashed through the soldiers until there were only five left standing.

"Shield!" yelled Antiope.

Diana watched as Menalippe grabbed a shield in both hands and held it parallel to the ground. Antiope jumped off her horse and ran toward Menalippe. Antiope jumped onto the shield and launched into the air. As Antiope soared closer to the German soldiers, she fired four arrows at once, killing all but one of the soldiers. The one remaining soldier raised his rifle and pointed it directly at Diana.

"Diana, look out!" yelled the pilot, as he pointed his gun at the German soldier.

The sound of two guns exploding filled the air. Less than a second later, the soldier crumpled to the ground. The pilot's bullet had killed him.

As Diana looked across the beach, strewn with lifeless bodies—Amazon and soldiers alike—she dropped to her knees and started sobbing. So many friends had sacrificed their lives, but why?

Hippolyta strode forward and pointed her hand at the pilot.

"You!" she said accusingly.

Diana looked up and protested, "Mother, no! He fought at my side against the invaders."

"Typical," said Antiope. "The man fights against his own people."

"They aren't *my* people!" the man protested.

"Then why do you wear a uniform of the same color as the invaders?" demanded Antiope.

"Tell us!" threatened Artemis, as she moved closer to the man.

He hesitated and said nervously, "I . . . I'm not at liberty to say."

"What is your name?" asked Phillipus.

"I can't tell you that, either," he said.

"We should kill him right now and be done with it," said Artemis.

"If he dies now, we know nothing about why they came here and who they are," argued Phillipus.

"Ladies, I'm sorry," said the man. "I can only tell you one thing about me: *I'll never talk!*"

SIX

Later that day, the queen ordered her closest advisers to join her in the throne room of the royal palace. Hippolyta sat on her throne and watched as Diana and four other Amazons formed a circle around the airline pilot. Antiope held a glowing, golden rope in her hands. The other end of the rope was tied tightly around the pilot, who struggled to free himself. Against his will, he began to speak.

"My name is Captain Steve Trevor," he said. "I'm a pilot. American Expeditionary Forces. Serial number 8121941. That's all I'm at liberty to say. . . ."

Antiope gave a tug on the lasso, which tightened around the pilot.

"I've been working for British Intelligence," he said reluctantly.

Steve Trevor glanced down at the glowing rope that held him and asked, "What is this thing, anyway?"

Diana stepped forward and said, "The Lasso of Hestia compels you to reveal the truth."

"It is pointless—and painful—to resist," added Antiope.

"What is your mission?" asked Queen Hippolyta.

"Whoever you are, you're in enough danger as it is. You shouldn't . . . *ouch*!" Steve cried out as the lasso tightened again.

"*What is your mission?*" demanded Hippolyta.

Steve sighed unhappily and then admitted, "I'm a spy. British Intelligence got word that the leader of the German army, General Ludendorff, was visiting a secret military installation in the Ottoman Empire. I posed as one of their pilots, then flew in with them."

Steve took a deep breath and then continued,

"According to our intelligence, the Germans had no troops left, no money, no munitions of any kind. But our reports were wrong. The Germans had the Turks making bombs for them. And not just bombs. They were making new weapons that were invented by Ludendorff's chief psychopath, Doctor Isabel Maru. The boys in the trenches call her 'Doctor Poison.' She was working on a deadly gas that could actually melt a gas mask and kill a person within seconds. From what I saw, if Doctor Maru was able to complete her work, millions would die. The war would never end. *I had to do something!*"

The Amazons looked at each other with puzzled faces.

Steve continued, "I snuck into the lab where she was working, and I stole her notebook. It contained the formula for her poison gas. I jumped into a plane and was on my way back to London when the Germans shot me down over your island."

He stared at his leather bag, which was on the floor, inches away from Hippolyta's throne. Diana reached into the bag and removed a small notebook.

Steve said, "But if I can get those notes to British Intelligence in time, it might make a difference . . . stop millions more from dying . . . stop the war . . ."

"War? What war?" asked Diana.

Steve turned to face her and said, "The war to end all wars. It started in 1914. It's been going on for four years. Twenty-seven nations, twenty-five million dead. Soldiers and civilians . . . innocent people . . ."

His voice trailed off with sadness, and then he continued, "Women and children slaughtered. Their homes and villages looted and burned. Weapons deadlier than you can imagine. Like nothing I've ever seen. It's like . . . *like the world is going to end.*"

"Take him to the infirmary," said Hippolyta sternly.

As two Amazon guards led Steve from the room, the other Amazons gathered around their queen.

"Should we let him go?" asked Phillipus.

"And risk him bringing more men to our shores?" said Hippolyta. "Phillipus, we should—"

"Mother—" Diana interrupted.

"We can't hold him forever, my queen," said Phillipus.

"Excuse me, Mother. But after everything the man said, how can we doubt what we should do? The man called it a war *without end*. Millions of people already dead. Like nothing he's ever seen. We cannot simply let him go. We must go with him."

Hippolyta stared at her daughter and said, "We are not deploying our army and leaving Themyscira defenseless to go and fight their war!"

"It is not *their* war," replied Diana. "You are the one who taught me that Zeus created man to be just and wise, strong and passionate."

"That was a *story*, Diana," said Hippolyta. "There is much you *do not know*. Mankind is easily corruptible. We must cater to our wounded, honor our fallen!"

"Themyscira has seen death for the first time, Mother," said Diana. "Ares must not be allowed to threaten us again. We know only too well what happens if he finds us. And now mankind must be freed. As Amazons, this is our duty!"

"You don't know war like we do," said Hippolyta,

her voice rising in anger.

"You may be afraid of war, Mother, but *I* am not," Diana challenged.

"Afraid? You know *nothing* of fear, child!" shouted Hippolyta. "*Nothing* of war. *Nothing* of pain. *Nothing* of sacrifice. So you will do nothing. *Your queen forbids it!*"

SEVEN

Under Queen Hippolyta's orders, Steve Trevor had been confined to his room in the infirmary. An Amazon healer named Epione was stationed outside the door. The next morning, she looked up as Diana approached.

"Is it true you saved his life?" asked Epione.

"He told you that?" asked Diana.

"He did," replied Epione. "What will the queen do with him? Will she kill him?"

Diana didn't answer. Instead, she silently turned

and entered the room. She was startled to see Steve Trevor stepping out of a bathtub. He was using a towel to dry himself when he suddenly heard a noise behind him. Steve spun around to see Diana. He hastily wrapped the towel around his waist.

"Didn't hear you come in," he said with annoyance. "Didn't hear you *knock*."

Diane eyed him with curiosity. Then she pointed to his wrist and asked, "What is that?"

"It's a watch."

"A watch," she repeated.

"My father gave it to me," said Steve. "It's been through everything with him, and now me, and it's still ticking."

Diana leaned forward to listen to the ticking of the watch and asked, "Why?"

"Because it tells time. So I know when to wake up, work, eat, sleep."

Diana asked with astonishment, "You let this little thing tell you what to do?"

Steve sighed and then said, "Do you mind if I ask you a couple hundred questions? What is this place?"

"Themyscira," replied Diana.

"I caught that before. I mean, what *is* this place? How come I've never heard of it? Who are you people? How do you all know English?"

"We speak hundreds of languages," said Diana. "We are the bridge to a greater understanding between all men."

Steve shook his head and said, "Funny, because I understand even less than before you walked in. But, hey, I didn't get to say it earlier, but thanks for dragging me out of the water."

Diana smiled and said, "Thank you for what you did on the beach."

"So . . . are you here to let me go?" asked Steve.

"I'm sorry. It's not up to me," said Diana. "I tried. I even asked them to send me with you . . . or anyone. An Amazon. The Amazons."

"The Amazons?" repeated Steve.

"It is our sacred duty to defend the world . . . and I wish to go. But my mother will not allow it."

Steve nodded and said, "Can't say I blame her. The way the war is going, I wouldn't let anyone *I* care about near it."

Diana was puzzled.

"Then why do you want to go back?" she asked.

Steve thought for a moment and then said, "I don't think *want* is the right word, but . . . I've gotta try. My father used to say, 'You see something wrong in the world, you can either do nothing, or you can do something. And you already tried nothing.'"

Diana pondered the words that Steve had just spoken.

You can *do something*, she thought to herself.

EIGHT

Later that night, Diana made her way through the dark and deserted streets of Themyscira. She ran quietly toward a tall stone tower at the edge of town. The Amazon armory was located inside that tower, and Diana knew that it contained a vast collection of weapons and valuable items.

Diana silently climbed a hillside next to the tower and hung back in the shadows. She glanced up at a single window at the top, several hundred feet above the ground. Two Amazons guarded the large wooden door at the base of the tower. Diana pondered her options. She could try to overpower the guards, but they were sure to call for help. She could jump from her hidden spot on the hillside, but the tower seemed so far away.

With a determined sigh, Diana decided that she would have to jump. She started sprinting toward the edge of the hillside, one step faster than the other. She reached the edge of the hill and leaped over the abyss below her. She soared through the nighttime air, a smile of satisfaction on her face. The smile quickly turned to a frown as the dark tower loomed in front of her. She slammed into the side of the tower and frantically grasped at the rough stones in the wall with her hands until she found a place to take hold. She took a few moments to catch her breath, and then she looked up. The window was at least thirty feet above her.

Gritting her teeth, Diana started to climb up the tower. She realized that by swinging her fist powerfully at the stone, she could create a handhold that allowed her to climb up the tower. Minutes later, she flipped herself up onto the ledge of the window and climbed into the room.

It took Diana's eyes a few moments to adjust to the moonlit darkness of the deserted armory. There she saw a shining silver sword hung majestically inside an intricate golden spiral dome. The sword glittered in the dark room, and she was awed by its sheer power.

Diana moved quickly through the room, grabbing a shield from a suit of ancient armor. The golden Lasso of Hestia was hanging on a nearby hook, and Diana carefully removed it. Next was an Amazonian battle suit, glowing in the dark room with its gold, red, and blue colors. Diana smiled as she slipped it on. She'd never felt a clearer purpose.

Back in the infirmary, Steve looked up in surprise as Diana entered.

"Nice outfit," he said as he admired her new armor.

"Thank you," said Diana. "Now I will show you the way off the island. And you will take me to the war."

Steve reached for his leather bag and his watch.

"Deal," he replied.

Soon, Diana and Steve were riding on horseback through the forest, heading toward the harbor. When they arrived at the shore, Steve was dismayed to see the ancient wooden sailing vessel that was moored in the water.

"I'm leaving in that?" he asked skeptically.

"*We* are," said Diana.

"*We're* leaving in that?" asked Steve.

Diana looked at him with scorn and asked, "Do you not know how to sail?"

"Of course I know how to sail," Steve protested. "Why wouldn't I be able to sail? I just haven't done it since I was a *kid*."

"Then there's nothing to be afraid of," Diana said matter-of-factly.

Suddenly, the thundering sound of approaching horses filled the air. Hippolyta was the first to arrive, followed by her Queen's Guard. She raised her hand, ordering the guards to halt. She dismounted and approached Diana alone.

Diana took a deep breath and moved toward her mother. She stared directly into Hippolyta's eyes and then spoke in a loud and clear voice.

"I can't stand by while innocent lives are lost," she said. "If no one else will defend the world from this war, I must. I have to go. . . ."

"I know," said Hippolyta, as a look of sadness filled her face. "Or at least, I know that I cannot stop you. There is so much . . . so much you do not understand."

Diana reached out to touch her mother's shoulder.

"I understand enough," said Diana. "That I'm willing to fight for those who cannot fight for themselves. Like you once did . . ."

Hippolyta stared at her daughter and said, "You know that if you choose to leave us, you may never return."

Diana nodded slowly. Hippolyta raised her hands and placed a glittering gold headband on her daughter's forehead. A shining star was located in the center of the headband.

"This belonged to one of the greatest warriors in our history," said Hippolyta. "Make sure that you are worthy of it."

"I will," said Diana.

As Diana and Steve stepped into the small wooden

boat, Hippolyta called out, "Be careful in the world of men, Diana. They do not deserve you."

Hippolyta watched as the boat sailed from the harbor. Soon, it was a small speck on the horizon. The queen continued to gaze at the water.

"You have been my greatest love," Hippolyta said softly. "Today, you are my greatest sorrow." She stood on the shore until the boat and its wake were no longer in sight.

NINE

A cold wind swept over Diana and Steve as they sailed across the Aegean Sea. Diana brushed the hair from her eyes and took a deep breath as her island home of Themyscira disappeared in the distance. She watched as it was swallowed up by the gray fog that surrounded it. Behind her, Steve struggled with the tiller. He was doing his best, but it was clear that he wasn't an expert sailor.

"How long until we reach the war?" she asked.

"The war?" Steve said with surprise. "Well, which

part? The Western Front in France alone is four hundred miles long. Then there is the Eastern Front and Italian Front, and of course all the fighting happening at sea and in the air."

Diana sighed with impatience and said, "Where the fighting is the most *intense* then. If you take me there, I am sure I can end this war."

"Look, *princess*, I like your spirit, and maybe you know something I don't, but this war is so sprawling there's nothing the two of us can do about it. But we *can* try to get to the men who can."

"You're looking at the person who can end this war," Diana said with confidence.

Steve raised an eyebrow and said, "I'm starting to understand why your mother didn't want you to leave. How much do you *really* know about the rest of the world?"

"The world of *men*?" Diana replied. "I know *all* that there is to know from the great books."

"The great books," Steve repeated slowly. "Do those books explain why there are no men on your island? Or kids?"

"*I* was raised on the island," Diana said.

"Just you?" Steve asked. "Must have been a sheltered upbringing."

"My mother sculpted me from clay," Diana explained. "I was brought to life by Zeus."

"Oh. Well, that's not how babies are made where I come from," said Steve.

Diana turned away to stare at the gray sky. She believed she was doing the right thing, but still, the farther she got from her home, the more she hoped she could really bring peace to mankind. It was her one great mission—what she'd given up her family and her home for. And she still wanted to make her mother proud.

The sailing was slow and arduous. Steve constantly scanned the horizon, searching for a ship that might help speed their journey. Eventually, they encountered a British steam ship that was headed to England. Steve and Diana happily climbed on board, and less than a week later they pulled into the port of London.

"We made good time," said Steve, as the ship docked. "Welcome to jolly old London."

Diana frowned as she viewed the sprawling, noisy city. Decaying buildings lined the wharf. In the distance, tall dark towers belched dark, sulfurous smoke into the air.

"It's hideous," she declared.

"Well, it's not for everyone," admitted Steve.

He quickly led Diana from the harbor to the heart of the city. Her eyes grew wider as she watched the horse-drawn carriages, the people wearing layers of fancy clothing, the cobblestone streets, and the newsstand vendors shouting out headlines about the war and voting rights for women. The smell of fresh bread and pastries from a bakery brought a smile to her face. The sour stench of freshly slaughtered meat from a butcher shop caused her to hold her nose. As Diana stopped to marvel at each distraction, Steve was constantly forced to grab her arm and propel her along.

Suddenly, she stopped in the middle of a busy road and was almost run over by an automobile. The driver of the car honked his horn and swerved around Diana.

"Diana!" yelled Steve.

Diana pointed to a woman and man who were holding hands. Diana looked confused. Steve pulled her onto the sidewalk.

"Why are they holding hands?" she asked.

Steve looked at the couple and said, "Well, because they're . . . together."

Diana nodded in comprehension, and reached over to grasp Steve's hand.

"No, *we're* not together," said Steve, as he quickly pulled his hand away. "I mean, not like that . . . I mean . . ."

Steve pointed down the street and said, "Look, we need to go *this* way."

Diana walked beside him and asked, "Because *this* is the way to the war?"

Steve reluctantly pointed in the other direction and said, "Technically, *that* is the way to the war."

"Then where are we going?" asked Diana.

"I have to get this notebook to my superiors."

Diana frowned and said, "I let you go, *you* take me to the war. We made a deal, Steve Trevor. A promise is unbreakable."

Steve sighed and said, "Oh boy. Okay. Come with

me to deliver this. Then we'll talk about getting you a train ticket."

As they continued to walk down the busy street, men and women openly stared at both Steve and Diana. Steve realized that although Diana was wearing a cloak that mostly covered her Amazon armor, the sight of her bare legs was quite shocking, even in a sophisticated city like London.

Steve said, "We need to cover your legs. I mean, we need to get you some clothes."

"Why?" asked Diana with surprise.

"Because you aren't wearing enough clothes," explained Steve.

Diana pointed to the women all around her. They were all wearing long skirts that reached the ground, and blouses that covered them from neck to wrist.

"What do *these* women wear into battle?" she asked.

Steve shrugged and said, "Well, women don't exactly . . ."

Before he could finish his sentence, Diana turned around to admire a woman carrying a baby.

"A baby," she said with wonder.

"And *that one* wasn't made out of clay," Steve said, as he gently took Diana by the arm and nudged her down the street toward the Selfridges and Company department store.

Just outside the store's entrance, a woman's voice called out. "It's true! You *are* alive!" she said.

Steve smiled as the woman approached them and reached out her arms to hug him. She was a short but strong woman, with curly brown hair, bright eyes, and a wide smile. Steve winced for a moment as she squeezed him tightly.

"Well, thank goodness for that!" she said happily. "I thought you were dead this time, I really did. And then I got your call."

The woman turned to Diana and said with exasperation, "He was gone for weeks! Not a word. Very unlike him."

She reached to clasp Diana's hand and said, "Hello, I'm Etta Candy. Captain Trevor's secretary."

Diana smiled and asked, "What is a secretary?"

Etta pondered the question for a moment and then said, "Well, it means I do everything. I go wherever he goes. Do whatever he tells me to do."

"Where I'm from, that's called slavery," Diana replied.

"Ooh, I *like* this one," Etta said with a smile. "It *does* rather feel like that sometimes. But the pay is good, and he's almost never here."

A breeze momentarily stirred Diana's cloak, exposing her bare legs and Amazon armor. Etta's eyes widened.

"Captain Trevor mentioned something about getting you a new outfit," she said, as she led Diana into the store. "We've got our work cut out for us."

As they walked through the store, Diana's mouth dropped open as she saw a heavy corset that had been draped around a mannequin. She reached out her hand to touch the stiff ribs that had been sewn inside the undergarment.

"Is that what passes for armor in your country?" she asked.

Etta smiled and said, "Of a sort. It's a fashion. Keeps our tummies in."

"Why must you keep them in?" asked Diana, puzzled.

"Only a woman with no tummy would ask that question!" replied Etta, as she hurried Diana through the store. "Let's go, dear."

When they reached the women's clothing department, Etta held up a heavy, dark-blue cloth dress.

"Conservative, but not entirely . . . unfun," offered Etta.

Diana viewed the thick fabric, long sleeves, and flowing skirt with dismay. She turned to Steve with a puzzled look on her face.

"At least try it on," Steve suggested.

Diana sighed and reached up to remove her cloak. It fell to the floor. Customers in the shop turned to stare at Diana's bare arms and legs. Etta quickly moved to place the cloak back on Diana's shoulders.

"Oh my," said Etta nervously. "Aren't you terribly cold out here where everyone can see . . . everything? Let's get you into a nice, warm, *private* dressing room, shall we?"

An hour later, with eight discarded dresses piled on the floor, Etta watched wearily as Diana modeled another outfit. She stood in front of a mirror, dressed from neck to toe in a bright-pink dress. Lacy white ruffles extended from the sleeves and collar to cover her neck and wrists. Diana glared at her reflection in a mirror.

"How can a woman possibly *fight* in this?" she asked.

"We fight with our principles," said Etta with a smile. "It's how we are going to get the right to the vote. Not that I'm opposed to engaging in a bit of fisticuffs when the situation calls for it, mind you!"

Etta handed Diana another dress and said, "Here we are. Very nice."

"So itchy," said Diana, when she emerged from the dressing room. "And it's choking me."

Under her breath, Etta said, "I can't say that I blame it."

Steve soon rejoined them. He was now wearing a handsome gray suit. His leather bag hung from his shoulder.

"How's it going?" he asked Etta.

"She's trying on outfit number two hundred and twenty-six," replied Etta.

Diana emerged from the dressing room, this time wearing a simple gray suit. Although the outfit was not showy, it suited Diana perfectly. Other customers looked up, struck by her beauty.

"Why is everyone staring?" asked Diana. "Is it because I can barely breathe in this suit?"

Steve could not stop looking at Diana.

"Etta, the whole point was to make her less *conspicuous*," he whispered.

Etta sighed and grabbed a pair of glasses from a nearby display. She gently placed the glasses on Diana's face.

"Really, Steve? All it takes is a pair of specs, and suddenly she's *not* the most beautiful woman you've ever seen?" Etta asked skeptically.

Diana studied her reflection. Against her better judgment, she decided that she would wear this new outfit. She even smiled a bit as she adjusted her new glasses.

"Here, dear, you're going to need this winter coat," said Etta, as she offered Diana a heavy wool coat.

Diana followed Etta and Steve to the front of

the store. When no one was looking, Diana quickly tucked her golden lasso inside her coat.

Outside the store, Etta turned to Diana and reached for her sword.

"Right, then. Good luck," she said. "I'll take this sword back to the office and meet you both later."

Diana frowned and yanked the sword from Etta's hands.

"It *really* doesn't go with the outfit," said Etta.

"It'll be safe," Steve reassured Diana. "You can trust her, I promise."

Reluctantly, Diana let Etta take the sword.

"Please," pleaded Diana. "Protect it with your life."

Etta raised an eyebrow and muttered quietly as she walked away, "Who wouldn't?"

Just then, Steve grabbed Diana's wrist and pulled her away from the front of the store and into a deserted alley.

"Come on," he said, quickening his pace.

Diana looked around in confusion and asked, "What is it?"

"Hopefully nothing," said Steve.

When they reached the end of the alley, five men suddenly appeared, blocking Steve and Diana from going anywhere. One of the men pointed a gun directly at Steve.

"Captain Trevor," he said. "I believe that you have something that is the property of General Ludendorff."

The other four men removed guns from their coats.

"Quite a reception," said Steve.

"Give us Doctor Maru's notebook . . . *now!*" said the man.

Steve stepped in front of Diana and patted the pockets of his coat as well.

"Where *did* I put that thing?" he said.

Steve lunged forward to kick his leg in the air. He knocked a gun out of the first man's hand. The man toppled against the other four men, who were still pointing their guns directly at Steve and Diana. Steve raised his arm to protect Diana.

"Stay behind me!" he ordered.

The four men fired their guns at the same time. The sound of the explosions echoed down the alley.

Steve watched with dismay as Diana jumped in front of him.

"No . . . Diana!" he yelled.

Diana raised her arms, exposing the silver bracelets on her wrists. The bullets bounced off the bracelets and ricocheted against a brick wall. The astonished men paused for a moment, and then they resumed firing. Diana continued to deflect the bullets with her bracelets.

Steve reached out to punch the first man and knocked him to the ground. The other four men charged toward Diana and Steve. Diana grabbed one of the men and swung him through the air. She then sent him crashing against two of the men. At the same time, Steve knocked the fourth man unconscious with a blow to the head.

Steve turned to Diana with a stunned look on his face and asked, "How did you *do* that?"

Diana looked behind her to see one of the men escaping down the alley. He darted around the corner and ran onto the main road.

"He's getting away . . . ," began Diana.

CLANG!

Diana and Steve ran to the corner. There they saw the man sprawled on the street, groaning in pain. Etta Candy stood over him. She held Diana's sword in her hands.

"I thought he looked suspicious," Etta said, with a satisfied smile.

TEN

Steve breathed a sigh of relief when he and Diana arrived at the British War Office without any more incidents. Together, they entered a large, wood-paneled room where several dozen men stood in small groups, each talking louder than the other. Among them were military leaders and members of Parliament. Steve escorted Diana to one corner of the room.

"Stay here . . . please," he said. "I need to meet with Colonel Darnell over there."

Steve walked past a tall, distinguished-looking man with gray hair and a kind face. He was impeccably dressed in a dark three-piece business suit and carried a cane. As Steve made his way over to speak with Colonel Darnell, Diana studied the room with fascination.

Steve leaned over to whisper in Colonel Darnell's ear. A surprised expression filled the man's face as Steve spoke with him.

Suddenly, Steve became aware that the room had gone silent. He glanced up to see that every man in the room was staring at Diana. She was the only woman in the room. Steve had forgotten that women were not allowed in the War Office.

Angrily, Colonel Darnell turned to Steve.

"Trevor? What were you thinking bringing a woman into the council chamber?"

"I'm sorry, Colonel Darnell," said Steve. "But the intel I've brought back is very time sensitive. We were attacked by men looking for it on the way here. I have one of Maru's notebooks."

Steve removed the notebook from his bag and continued, "We need to get this to Cryptography. And

I need an immediate audience with the generals. . . ."

Colonel Darnell frowned and said, "You don't just rush in here like this and demand an audience with the *cabinet*. Cryptography takes time and—"

"Captain Trevor," interrupted Sir Patrick, as he joined the two men. "Welcome back. I'd heard you were lost on one of your missions, yet here you are. And you've brought a friend."

Sir Patrick nodded toward Diana, who smiled back at him.

Colonel Darnell turned to Sir Patrick and said, "Our deepest apologies for this interruption, Sir—"

"Nonsense," said Sir Patrick. "Thanks to this young woman, the room was finally quiet enough for me to get a few words in."

Steve groaned inwardly as Diana crossed the room and joined the three men.

"Sir Patrick Morgan, at your service," said the older man, as he bowed to Diana.

"Diana, princess of . . . ," she began.

"Prince, Diana Prince," Steve quickly interrupted. "We . . . she and I . . . we work together. She helped me get the notebook here. From Doctor Maru's lab."

Steve handed the notebook to Sir Patrick, who started leafing through it.

"Doctor Poison's notebook? My God," he said, as he turned to Colonel Darnell. "I suggest we assemble the members of the War Cabinet so they can tell us more."

Darnell hesitated for a moment, and then he reluctantly nodded.

Later that day, Steve and Diana stood in front of a large group of men in another room in the War Office. Sir Patrick Morgan and Colonel Darnell were there, along with General Douglas Haig and members of the British War Cabinet. The walls of the room were covered with maps, along with photos of the German General Ludendorff and Doctor Maru.

Colonel Darnell handed the notebook back to Steve.

"Cryptographers had no luck," said Darnell. "It seems like a mixture of two languages."

Diana leaned forward to peer at the notebook and said, "Ottoman and Sumerian."

Everyone in the room turned to look at Diana with astonished looks on their faces.

"What?" asked Diana. "Surely someone else in this room knew that."

"Who *is* this woman?" asked General Haig.

"She's my . . . secretary," offered Steve.

At the sound of the word *secretary*, Diana turned to glare at Steve, but he gave her a look that said now was not the time to argue with him.

"And she speaks Ottoman and Sumerian?" asked Haig.

"She's a very good secretary," said Steve.

"See her out," ordered Haig.

"If this woman can read it, sir, perhaps we should hear what she has to say," said Darnell.

Diana nodded to Darnell and said, "Thank you. It's a formula . . . for a new kind of mustard . . ."

Haig snorted and said sarcastically, "Mustard?!"

Diana, ignoring the rude interruption, calmly continued. "Mustard *gas*. Hydrogen-based, instead of sulfur."

Darnell gasped and said, "Gas masks would be *useless* against hydrogen."

Princess Diana is an Amazon living on a secret island called Themyscira. Queen Hippolyta is her mother. General Antiope and Menalippe are her aunts. They are not only wise and noble, but also incredible warriors.

Diana and her mother, Queen Hippolyta, listen to Steve Trevor's account of the war to end all wars. Diana wants to join the fight, but the queen forbids her to go.

Diana sneaks into the armory, where the Amazons keep their weapons. She finds a powerful sword that will help her in her mission to save mankind.

When Diana arrives in London, she has to learn to fit in. Steve Trevor helps her find a disguise.

Diana, Steve, Charlie, and Sameer discuss their mission to find General Ludendorff and Doctor Maru.

Steve's secretary, Etta Candy, assists the team. While the group plans to head to the front, Etta gathers information for their mission.

General Ludendorff plans to release a powerful weapon that will greatly impact the outcome of the war.

Doctor Maru is hard at work on her experiment to help the Germans win the war.

Diana prepares for her encounter
with General Ludendorff at the Gala.

Captain Steve Trevor heroically pilots the stolen aircraft through enemy attacks.

Diana surprises the enemy with her expert combat skills.

Diana and Steve make a great team. They plot how to get into a gala where Diana can confront the enemy and end the war.

Diana dons her final disguise before confronting the enemy at General Ludendorff's gala. She is ready to fight for peace.

Diana studied the book and said, "It says that they plan to release this gas at . . . the Front."

She paused in confusion and looked over at Steve.

"The front of what?" she asked.

Steve turned to General Haig and said, "Sir, you *have* to find out where they are making this gas. Burn it to the ground. Destroy it!"

"Ludendorff was last seen in Belgium," said Darnell.

"I can't risk sending more troops into German-occupied Belgium with only this notebook as evidence," said Haig.

"Sir, I saw this *gas* with my own eyes," Steve said. "All the men on the front line could die on *both sides* unless you—"

"That's what soldiers *do*, Captain," barked Haig. "Would you have us abandon the Front altogether?"

"Pull the troops out," said Steve. "Send me in. With some strategic support, I could take Ludendorff and his operation out *myself*."

"Are you *insane*, Trevor?" said Haig. "I can't introduce rogue elements this late into the game."

"But, General—" began Steve.

"You will do *nothing*, Captain Trevor. *That is an*

order!" Haig commanded.

As Diana watched in disbelief, Steve bowed his head and said quietly, "Yes, sir. I understand, sir."

"*I* don't!" declared Diana.

Steve turned to her and whispered, "Diana, I know it's confusing."

"It's not confusing," said Diana. "It's *unthinkable*!"

Haig turned to stare at Diana and said, "I'm sorry, *who* did you say this *woman* was?"

"She's with me. With *us*," said Steve, as he reached forward to pull Diana back.

"I am *not* with you!" she said, as she angrily broke away from Steve and turned to glare at Haig. "You would knowingly sacrifice all those lives? Do they mean less than yours? Where I come from, generals don't hide in their offices like cowards. They fight alongside their soldiers. They *die* with them on the battlefield."

"Diana. *Enough!*" yelled Steve, as he turned to face Haig. "My apologies, sir."

Diana spun around to face Steve.

"You should be ashamed," she shouted, as she

stormed out of the room. "*All* of you!"

Steve quickly exited the War Office. He found Diana in a rage, pacing back and forth in the hallway.

"*That* is your leader?" she shouted. "How could he say that? *Believe* that? And *you*! Was your duty to simply give them a *book*? You didn't stand your ground! You didn't fight!"

Steve stepped closer to her and said, "Because there was no chance of changing his mind. Listen to me. . . ."

"The millions of people you talked about?" Diana said. "They will die. My people? They're next!"

"If you will just listen to me . . ."

"How can you call yourselves good men?" Diana asked.

Steve grabbed her shoulders and shouted, "*We're going anyway!*"

Diana grew quiet. She studied Steve's face.

"What? You mean you were lying?" she asked.

"Diana, I'm a spy," Steve said. "That's what we *do*. Now, are you coming or not?"

Diana frowned and asked, "How do I know you're

not lying to me right now?"

Steve reached forward and wrapped Diana's golden lasso around his wrist. It started to glow.

"The truth is that I'm taking you to the Front. If we're going to get to the Front on our own, we're going to need reinforcements."

ELEVEN

Later that night, Diana walked closely behind Steve as he led her down a dark and winding street at the edge of the city. They came to a dilapidated building that Steve described to her as a "pub." When he opened the door, Diana peered inside the dimly lit room. She saw two dozen or so men, all wearing ill-fitting clothes and smelling of sweat. Several were engaged in heated arguments, and two men in the corner were throwing punches at each other.

"*These* are your reinforcements?" she asked. "Are these even good men?"

"*Relatively* good," admitted Steve.

Diana raised an eyebrow and asked, "Relative to what?"

A well-dressed young man was sitting at a table near the door. He was talking nonstop to two British officers. His bright eyes shone, and he occasionally raised his eyebrows or twitched his mustache to emphasize a point he was making.

"In Africa, gentlemen, we had *no* such luxuries," the man said with a broad smile.

The two officers laughed and nodded their heads in agreement.

"But the luxuries we have now," the man continued, as he leaned closer to speak to the two men. "It's like we can't stop making money. My uncle, the prince, and I would keep it all, but we want to extend the opportunity to a few good soldiers. . . ."

Steve reached over and placed his hand on the man's shoulder.

"And which prince *was* that?" Steve said loudly, as he tightened his grip on the man's shoulder. "I need to talk to you, Prince Madras Angora Cashmere. . . ."

The man grinned nervously and stood up, after excusing himself to the two surprised officers. He followed Steve and Diana to the other side of the pub.

"You jerk," the man said to Steve. "I've been greasing those peacocks all night, and then you come along to spoil my . . ."

He stopped midsentence and glanced at Diana.

"My goodness gracious, *that's* a work of art," he said with admiration.

"Sameer, this is Diana," said Steve.

Sameer smiled broadly and said, "Diana, call me Sammy. Please."

"Sammy. Please," replied Diana.

"Sammy is a top undercover man," Steve explained. "He can talk the skin off a cat in as many languages as you."

Diana eyed Sammy warily and said in Spanish, "He doesn't look that impressive to me."

Sammy instantly responded in Spanish, "You do to me. Your eyes, as soft as your smile . . ."

Diana switched to Chinese. "And your eyes look like they want something."

"I know Chinese too, tricky girl," Sammy replied in Chinese.

Diana next tried ancient Greek. "But can you recite Socrates in ancient Greek?"

Sammy opened his mouth and then quickly closed it. Diana had stumped him.

"Where's Charlie?" asked Steve.

Sammy pointed to the corner of the pub where the two men were fighting. A large, angry-looking man was beating up a much smaller man. The smaller man cowered against the bar, shifting his arms over his body to avoid the blows. Diana nodded approvingly at the large man.

"At least this Charlie is good with his *fists*," she said.

"That's not Charlie," said Steve.

BLAM!

The large man threw a punch that knocked his smaller opponent to the floor.

Steve walked over to help the little man get back on his feet.

"*This* is Charlie," he said to Diana.

A few minutes later, Steve and Diana were sitting around a table with Sammy and Charlie. Diana looked apprehensive.

"Are you okay, Charlie?" asked Steve.

In a thick Scottish brogue, Charlie replied, "Ah, Steven! May God put a flower on your head."

"What were you fighting about?" asked Diana.

"I mistook his drink for mine," Charlie admitted cheerfully.

Diana turned to Steve and said, "This man is no fighter."

"Charlie here is an expert marksman," said Steve.

Diana looked puzzled, so Steve explained, "He shoots people."

"From very far away," added Sammy.

Charlie reached over to steal a drink from another table and raised it in Diana's direction.

"They never know what hits 'em," he boasted.

"How do you know who you *kill* if you can't see their faces?" Diana asked.

"I don't," said Charlie. "It's better that way."

Diana frowned and said, "My aunt warned me about men like you."

"Ain't the first time I've heard that, lassie," said Charlie.

Diana's face grew stern, and she said, "You fight without honor."

"Don't get paid for honor," replied Charlie.

Sammy leaned across the table and asked, "What's the job, Trevor?"

"Two days tops," said Steve. "We need supplies and passage to Belgium—"

"What's the going rate?" interrupted Charlie.

"Better be good pay," added Sammy.

He then turned to Diana and smiled, as he spoke in perfect French, "And perhaps a picture of your lovely face. Something to keep me alive."

Diana tried to hide her disdain as she replied in French, "You won't need a picture. I'm coming with you."

Sammy's smile faded instantly, and he turned to Steve. "What *is* this?" he asked.

"We're dropping her off at the Front," said Steve.

"Dropping her off?" Sammy repeated.

"No offense, darling," Charlie said to Diana, "but I don't wanna get killed helping a girl out of a ditch, if you know what I mean."

Suddenly, a giant hand clamped down on Charlie's shoulder. It was the large man who had fought with him earlier, and he held a gun in his other hand. Standing behind him were two equally large and angry men.

"You got your friends," said the large man, as he pushed the gun against Charlie's back. "These are my friends."

Before Charlie could even open his mouth, Diana jumped up from the table, grabbed the man's gun and reached over to grab the large man by the neck. She then easily picked him up and threw him across the room. The man crashed against the bar, causing glasses and bottles to come tumbling down on top of him. The man's friends quickly ran from the pub.

Sammy watched the proceedings in astonishment.

"I am both frightened *and* impressed," he said.

Just then, Etta Candy entered the pub.

"There you are," she said to Steve and Diana. "Hello, all! Sorry I'm late. I got waylaid by—"

"Sir Patrick!" said Diana, as the British gentleman entered the room.

"That's what I was going to mention," said Etta.

Steve, Sammy, and Charlie immediately stood up out of respect.

"Sit, gentlemen. Please, sit," said Sir Patrick. "I assume you're here planning something that's either going to get you court-martialed or killed."

Steve sighed and said, "I assume you're here to stop us."

"No," replied Sir Patrick. "Not that I like any of this. As one of your American authors, Thomas Paine, so eloquently put it, 'I prefer peace. But if trouble must come, let it come in my time, so that my children can live in peace.'"

Sir Patrick lowered his voice to a whisper and said, "I'm here to help you. Unofficially, of course. What's your plan?"

Steve spoke softly. "If there is another weapons facility, I plan to find it and destroy it. Along with Ludendorff and Maru."

Sir Patrick nodded and said, "Etta will run the mission out of my office, to allay suspicion."

Etta smiled and said happily, *"Run* the mission, sir?"

Sir Patrick removed an envelope from his pocket and discreetly handed it to Steve.

"It's enough for a few days," said Sir Patrick.

"Thank you, sir," said Steve, as he clasped Sir Patrick's hand. They were on their way to Belgium.

TWELVE

The next day, Diana and Steve made their way slowly through the crowds of people within London's Paddington Station. Every new sight—whether it was the station's arched metal roof or the arrival of a smoke-belching locomotive train—caused Diana to stop and stare. She turned to marvel at two men riding bicycles through the station. Her face saddened when she saw a little girl crying. She smiled when she saw a young couple embracing. Steve watched Diana's reactions closely. He enjoyed seeing the world through Diana's eyes.

"The train leaves in a few minutes," he said.

Diana didn't hear him. She was staring at a man and his daughter. They were happily eating two ice-cream cones.

Steve turned to Diana and asked, "Hungry?"

Diana nodded, and watched carefully as Steve purchased two ice-cream cones from a vendor. He handed one to Diana, and she tentatively ran her tongue over the ice cream.

"It's cold," she said with delight.

"It's ice cream," explained Steve.

A broad smile filled Diana's face, as she turned to the ice-cream vendor and said enthusiastically, "It's *wonderful*. You should be *very* proud!"

Steve tugged on her arm to move her in the direction of their train. He leaned in closer to Diana.

"Forget the countries or the territory or the generals," he said. "*This* is what we're really fighting for."

As they boarded the train, Diana paused to take one

final look at the throngs of people in the station. She took comfort knowing that her sword was now safely tucked within the folds of her scratchy undergarments. After she ended the war, she wondered if she would return here and begin a new life in London. Would she eat ice cream every day? She smiled at the thought.

Hours later, the train rattled to a stop in Dover. Diana peered through the sooty windows and looked at the wooden docks that stood at the edge of the gray water. Hundreds of soldiers were disembarking from the train, and Diana jumped from her seat, eager to join them.

Diana, Steve, Sammy, and Charlie exited the train and walked quickly toward the boarding ramp for a steamship. A large group of young soldiers, newly recruited to fight in the war, marched alongside them. The soldiers were singing. Diana paused, trying to decipher the lyrics. Steve gently pulled her arm to keep her moving.

"We've got to get going," he said. "Chief won't wait."

As they waited in line to board the ship, Diana turned to Steve and asked, "Chief?"

"Smuggler. Very reputable," replied Steve.

Diana raised an eyebrow and said, "A liar, a murderer, and now a smuggler?"

"Careful. I might get offended," replied Steve with a smile.

Diana frowned and said, "I wasn't referring to you."

"I went undercover and pretended to be someone else," Steve said. "I shot people on your beach, and I smuggled a notebook. Liar, murderer, smuggler."

He reached out his hand to her and stepped onto the ship's boarding ramp.

"You still coming?" he asked.

Diana nodded firmly. She and her companions quickly boarded the ship.

As the ship pulled out of port, Steve and Diana stood on the deck and surveyed the crowded docks. They saw nurses wearing soiled and bloody uniforms. The nurses were tending to dozens of wounded soldiers who had been carried on stretchers off the ship. The groans of the injured soldiers filled the air. Diana reached over to grasp Steve's arm. Both stood mute, watching the scene below them. They were headed to where the injured soldiers had come from.

Diana tried to sleep during the fourteen-hour journey to Belgium, but each time she closed her eyes she found herself thinking about the wounded soldiers in Dover. She anxiously ran her hand along the hilt of her sword. How soon would she be able to put it to use?

After the ship docked in Belgium, Diana and her companions waited on the deck as the soldiers disembarked. Diana's eyes widened as she saw horses in gas masks being led down the ramp.

"The gas will kill everyone, everything," she said to Steve. "What kind of weapon kills innocents?"

"In this war? Every kind," said Steve. "Come on. It's about an hour's hike to reach Chief."

They walked into a wooded area not far from the dock and made their way down a winding path through the forest. Diana inhaled deeply, taking in the smell of the rustling trees. With her sharp eyes, she spotted birds nestled in the branches and woodland animals peeping from their hiding places.

As nighttime approached, the four companions stepped cautiously out of the dark woods and into a clearing where a small campfire was burning. A tall man was standing in front of the fire, dropping logs into it. His back was to Steve and the others.

"You're late," said the tall man without turning around.

"Chief!" said Steve with relief.

The tall man turned around to face the four of them. He was a Native American, and his dark eyes sparkled in the glow of the campfire. His long black hair was pulled back tightly behind his head, and a small, bright feather was tucked into the headband of his hat.

"It's good to see you," said Sammy.

"Aye," agreed Charlie.

Chief looked at Diana and asked, "Who is this?"

Diana stepped forward and reached out her hand. Chief responded by solemnly grasping her wrist in a manner similar to the Amazons on Themyscira.

In his native tongue, Chief said, "*Niitangio, Napi.*"

Diana responded in the same Native American language, "I am Diana."

Chief laughed and asked, "Where did you find her?"

"She found me," Steve admitted.

Diana began to explain, "I plucked him from the sea when he—"

"It's a *long* story," interrupted Steve.

Diana glanced behind Chief and noticed a huge pile of packages on the ground. A few guns were scattered on top of the packages. She turned to Steve with a puzzled look on her face.

"British tea for the Germans," Steve said. "German spirits for the British. Edgar Rice Burroughs novels for both sides."

"And *guns*," said Charlie happily, as he reached forward to grab a rifle. He caressed the rifle tenderly against his chin.

Steve removed a map from his jacket and said, "Ludendorff was last seen at the Front near the Somme. The Front is about three miles away. Chief will get us there."

"Then it's another day to safely cross it," said Chief.

"As soon as we have daylight, we move," said Steve. "I'll take first watch."

Charlie held up a hand in protest as he sat down next to the fire.

"No need," he said. "I'll take it. I *never* sleep on the job!"

One hour later, Charlie was fast asleep, curled into a ball next to the fire. Steve and Sammy slumbered on the ground not far away. Diana and Chief sat by the fire, as Chief reached forward to heat a can of food. The booming sound of guns and heavy artillery could be heard in the distance.

Diana looked up and said, "Strange thunder."

"German seventy-sevens," said Chief.

Diana looked confused, so he explained, "Guns. Big ones. That's the Front out there. The evening hate."

Chief handed her a can of heated beans. She dipped a fork into it and tasted the beans. A pained look filled her face. This was not as tasty as ice cream.

Diana discreetly placed the can of beans on the

ground and watched Chief as he counted a large stack of money.

"So . . . ," she began cautiously, "who do you fight for in this war?"

Chief stuffed the money in his pocket and said, "I don't fight."

Diana frowned and said, "You're here for the *profit* then?"

"Nowhere better to be," replied Chief with a smile.

"Nowhere better to be than a war you don't take a side in?" challenged Diana.

Chief slowly turned to face Diana and said, "I have nowhere else and no side left. The last war took everything from my people. We have nothing left. At least here, I'm free."

"Who took that from your people?" Diana asked indignantly.

Chief pointed in the direction of the sleeping Steve Trevor and said simply, "*His* people."

Diana had no response to this. She sat quietly next to the campfire and stared at Steve in the flickering light of the flames.

Hours later, she was still lost in her thoughts when

Steve began to stir. He yawned, rubbed his eyes, and looked up to see Diana watching him.

"You're going to get cold," said Steve, as he offered her a blanket. "Here."

"I'm not cold," protested Diana, as Steve reached over to wrap the blanket around her shoulders. The warmth of the soft fabric caused her eyes to droop. She looked up at Steve and smiled at him. Minutes later, she was fast asleep.

THIRTEEN

Just miles away from Diana and her companions, a top-secret command station had been built in the middle of the Belgian battlefield. The German war council was meeting inside the building. That night, General Ludendorff paced around the room, angrily waving his arms. A tall man with close-cropped gray hair, his cheeks were flushed with rage. He turned to face his superior officer, Commander Von Hindenburg, who silently glared at Ludendorff.

A half-dozen German officers watched nervously in the background.

"We can easily *win* this war still," shouted Ludendorff. "If only you had *faith* in me!"

"But we *don't* have faith in you," said Von Hindenburg. "We have no choice but to retreat. There are shortages of food, medicine, and ammunition. Every hour we delay costs thousands of German lives."

"One attack and the war is ours," said Ludendorff. "As we speak, my chemist, Doctor Maru, and her team are—"

"We stand against you and your *witch*, Ludendorff!" barked Von Hindenburg. "Enough!"

Ludendorff stormed out of the building and slammed the door behind him. He walked up to a woman who was standing near the entrance. It was Doctor Maru, and her large, dark eyes widened with apprehension as he approached her. Ludendorff paused to gaze at Maru for a moment. He studied the three interlocking metal plates that covered the lower part of her face. Although the metal plates were flesh-colored, they gave her face a grotesque robotic look.

Maru quickly tugged at her coat collar with one hand in a futile attempt to hide her scars. She held a small metal canister in her other hand.

Ludendorff glanced down at the canister and smiled. He then reached back to open the door to the building.

"Do it," he said to Maru.

She quickly tossed the canister into the room. She then watched with surprise as Ludendorff reached over to grab a gas mask. He threw the mask into the room and then slammed the door shut and locked it.

"That gas mask won't help," said Maru.

"Yes, but *they* don't know that," said Ludendorff.

A hissing sound of leaking gas could be heard within the building. Seconds later, Ludendorff smiled as he listened to the anguished screams of the men and the sound of their hands beating against the locked door.

Soon, it grew silent. Ludendorff took Maru by the arm and led her away.

"It's time to stage our demonstration for the kaiser," he said.

The next morning, as the sun began to rise in the gray skies over Belgium, Diana and her companions made their way carefully down a country road. Chief was in the lead, and his eyes busily scanned the ground.

"You'll want to walk behind me," he said to Diana.

"And why is that?" she asked.

Chief gestured for Sammy to hand him a can. Chief then hurled the can into the middle of the road ahead of them.

BOOM!

The can detonated a land mine, causing an instant explosion.

"That's why," said Chief, as he resumed walking.

Diana fell in line behind him.

Two hours later, the gray skies darkened and rain began to fall. The road quickly turned to mud, causing Chief and his companions to slow their pace. Suddenly, the sound of bullets ricocheted above their heads. Diana and the others dropped to the muddy ground and crawled on their hands and knees to a nearby hole carved in the mud. They moved through the hole and entered a deep trench. British soldiers and frightened Belgian residents were crowded next to them within the trench.

"Where are we?" asked Diana.

"You wanted me to take you to the war," said Steve. "This is it. The front lines."

Diana was puzzled.

"But where are the Germans?" she asked.

Charlie pointed toward one end of the trench and said, "Couple hundred yards that way. In a trench like this one."

Diana frowned as she turned to view the seemingly endless line of British soldiers who were trudging wearily through the trench. The faces of the soldiers were filled with fear and fatigue.

Diana turned to a Belgian woman who was standing near her. The woman was young, and she was clutching her infant daughter close to her. Both mother and daughter were shivering, whether from fright or the cold Diana couldn't tell. Diana reached into Steve's duffel bag and removed the blanket. She offered it to the woman and child.

In a weary voice, the woman spoke to Diana in Dutch.

"The Germans took everything . . . homes and food," she said. "Our people who couldn't escape, the Germans took as slaves."

"Where did this happen?" Diana asked.

The woman pointed helplessly beyond the trench.

Diana turned to Steve and said, "We need to *help* these people."

"We *need* to stay on mission," replied Steve.

Chief nodded in agreement and said, "And there's no safe crossing ahead for at least a day."

"But these people are *dying*," Diana protested. "They have nothing to eat. And in the village . . . *enslaved*, she said! Women. Children."

She paused to look at her companions and asked, "Is there truly not *one* among you with honor?"

Steve turned to Diana and angrily said, "Thousands of men die on this line every day! So if you're looking for honor in *this* mess, you won't find any. I told you this war is—"

"Unlike any other," Diana interrupted. "So what? So we should do *nothing*?"

"We can't save every person in this war," said Steve.

"*We can try!*" Diana argued.

"We would *die* trying, Diana," said Steve. "There's a trench full of MG-08 machine guns and heavy artillery on the other side aimed at every square inch of this one. Between them: *no-man's-land*. It'll take this entire army *six months* to gain even an *inch*. Besides, it's not what we came here to do."

Diana stepped away from the group and began to climb up the side of the trench.

"No, but it's what *I'm* going to do," she said, as she jumped over the top of the trench and stood at the edge of the muddy battlefield.

"Diana! *No!*" yelled Steve.

Diana unsheathed her sword and held it aloft. The golden lasso at her side began to glow. She took a step forward.

Suddenly, a German soldier reached over the top of a trench. He pointed his gun directly at Diana and fired. At the sound of the explosion, Diana quickly lifted her left arm. The bullet bounced harmlessly off the silver bracelet around her wrist. The German soldier fired again, this time a fast succession of bullets.

Diana used her bracelets to knock away each bullet.

Back in the British soldiers' trench, Charlie poked his head over the top. His mouth fell open in astonishment.

"How did she do that?" he marveled.

Bullets were flying from dozens of German soldiers, but Diana easily swatted each bullet away as she walked across the battlefield. Her pace began to quicken. Soon, she started to run past the astonished German soldiers. Their bullets ricocheted harmlessly into the air.

Steve turned to his companions and called out, "She's drawing their fire! Let's go!"

With a yell, Steve and his companions jumped out of the trench and ran toward the Germans.

As the bullets continued to fly, a group of German soldiers scrambled to lift a heavy mortar. They pointed it directly at Diana.

BOOM!

Four explosive mortar shells soared through the air. Diana planted her feet firmly in the ground and lifted her shield.

KER-BLAM!

The mortar shells collided against Diana's shield and broke into tiny fragments. Diana was unharmed.

The British soldiers gave a loud cheer. Inspired by Diana's bravery, they surged over the top of their trench and joined the battle.

A German soldier pointed a machine gun at Diana and began to fire. Then a second machine gun opened fire on her. She crouched down to her knees and raised her bracelets to deflect the steady barrage of bullets. She realized with dismay that the combined fire of the two machine guns was slowing her progress into the battlefield.

As the bullets continued to soar, she heard a sound behind her. She turned her head and smiled. Steve and his friends, joined by the British soldiers, were charging forward toward her. Steve and Charlie aimed their rifles and took out a half-dozen German soldiers. Sammy grabbed a grenade from Chief and tossed it into the German trench. The exploding grenade destroyed one of the machine guns.

The second machine gun continued to fire at Diana. She started to run toward it and took a flying leap. She soared through the air and landed with a crash on top of a group of astonished German soldiers in their trench. Diana lifted her shield and then smashed it into the machine gun. The weapon crumbled into pieces.

Steve's team and the British forces followed Diana into the trench and quickly overpowered the German soldiers.

Steve turned to savor the moment of victory with Diana, but she was already climbing out of the trench. She began to run toward the nearby village of Veld, where the sound of German gunfire could be heard.

"We're not finished yet," she called out.

Steve and his team ran after her, stumbling down the muddy road.

Diana and her companions paused at the edge of the village. They crouched down as bullets flew over their heads.

"I'll go ahead," she said.

Before anyone could respond, Diana unsheathed her sword and ran toward the gunfire.

Steve lifted his rifle and fired. He motioned for the team to follow Diana.

"Go!" he shouted, as they scrambled after her.

Diana ran into the middle of the village and took a flying leap through the window of a building. Shards of glass crashed inside the room as Diana landed in the middle of a group of armed German soldiers. They immediately started to fire at Diana, as she kicked over a table and tossed it against two of the soldiers. As she deflected bullets with her bracelets, she cut one soldier with her sword. She then slammed her fists into two other soldiers. She used her shield to knock another soldier through the open window.

Steve and his team were standing in the street outside the building, and they watched with amazement as the German soldier landed on the ground in front of them. Seconds later, another dazed German soldier came flying through the window.

Chief handed Steve a grenade, and Steve tossed it behind a wall where a group of German soldiers were firing their guns. The exploding grenade instantly ended the German gunfire.

Diana crashed through the wooden door of the building. She ran down the street and jumped onto a stone wall. She then leaped onto a nearby rooftop. German soldiers surrounded the building and started firing on her from all sides. She deflected the bullets with her bracelets and gestured toward the front door of the building below her.

Steve and his companions looked over to see an anguished group of people inside the building, locked behind two wooden doors. They were people from the town of Veld, and they were crying out for help.

Steve threw two hand grenades, taking out a few of the German soldiers who were firing at Diana. His companions rushed forward to break open the wooden doors and free the townspeople.

Two German soldiers climbed onto the roof next to Diana, and she spun around to grab hold of them and slam their heads together. She then lifted both soldiers and tossed them aside.

More German soldiers continued to pour into Veld, and Diana looked up with alarm to see one soldier climbing a tall bell tower in the center of town. Steve looked up to follow her gaze and saw the man reach the top of the tower. Seconds later, a steady barrage of bullets shot out of the tower.

Diana ran down to join her companions.

"Charlie," Steve called out. "Sniper in the bell tower!"

Charlie pulled out his rifle and pointed it toward the tower. He squinted through the scope and fired. The bullet missed its target and instead ricocheted off the side of the bell inside the tower. The sniper instantly turned to face Steve and his companions and began firing at them.

"You *never* miss," said Sammy, as he and the others scrambled for cover.

"Bloody scope," muttered Charlie. "Lens is cracked."

"Is there a way inside the tower?" asked Diana.

"There is," Steve said, "if you jump!"

Diana looked up at the tower and said, "It's too high."

Steve bent down and picked up a piece of metal debris from the ground. He reached over and tapped her shield with his hand. A look of comprehension filled Diana's face. She suddenly remembered how Antiope had used her shield during the battle on Themyscira.

Steve held the metal plate parallel to the ground and motioned to Diana that he was ready. Diana began running toward Steve. She jumped up onto the plate and launched herself into the air.

The German sniper on top of the tower gritted his teeth and peered through the scope of his rifle, watching the activity below him. He tensed his finger and began to squeeze the trigger.

POW!

Diana's shield smashed into the sniper before he could fire his rifle. The man toppled over the edge of the tower and landed on a nearby rooftop. The few remaining German soldiers ran from the town square and were quickly captured by the British troops.

A loud cheer erupted from the grateful townspeople, as they slowly emerged from their battered buildings. Diana looked down from atop the bell tower, searching for Steve. He was standing by himself at the edge of the town square, staring up at her, a look of awe on his face.

It was nearing dawn, and Diana emerged from the tower to join Steve and his companions. A grateful photographer motioned for them to gather together in the town square so that he could take their picture.

The five teammates stood together in the center of

town. Their clothes were covered with mud, and their faces showed the weariness of the past day's battles. Diana stood in the middle of the group, a cloak barely covering her Amazon armor. A fierce look of determination filled her face. It was as if she knew that an even bigger battle still lay ahead of them.

FOURTEEN

Later that day, Steve and his teammates crowded into the lobby of a small inn. It was the only building in Veld that still had a working telephone.

"We're in Veld," Steve shouted into the phone. "Tiny village. It's probably not even on the—"

From the War Office in London, Etta Candy quickly interrupted Steve. "Found it," she said.

"Have you found Ludendorff's operation?" asked Steve.

"Not yet, but we've located Ludendorff," replied

Etta. "And *lucky you*, he's only a few miles away . . . at German High Command."

"German High Command?" repeated Steve.

"Intel reports that Ludendorff is hosting a gala tomorrow night," said Etta. "The kaiser himself will be there. As will Doctor Maru."

"Actually, the gala is a perfect cover," said Steve.

Sir Patrick's loud voice boomed through the phone.

"Captain Trevor, you are under no circumstances to attend that gala tomorrow," he said. "It's too risky."

"Sir, this is our chance to find the gas and learn how Ludendorff plans on delivering it," Steve argued. "It may be our only chance. Our *last* chance!"

"I forbid it," said Sir Patrick. "Do you hear me, Steve?"

Steve held his hand over the phone's receiver and said, "I'm sorry, sir. You're breaking up."

"Steve? Are you there . . . ?" yelled Sir Patrick, before Steve hung up the phone.

Steve turned to Sammy and said, "Sameer, I need you to rustle me up a German uniform."

"Already done," said Sammy. "Now you and Diana need to relax. There's nothing we can do until the party tomorrow night."

Steve looked up to see that Diana had stepped through the door. He stood up and followed her. He found her standing outside the inn, staring up at the sky with a puzzled look on her face. It had started to snow.

"It's a snowfall," explained Steve.

Diana's expression filled with wonder as she watched the snowflakes drifting to the ground.

"It's magical," she said with awe.

Steve smiled and said, "You're right. Would you care to dance?"

Diana gingerly nodded yes, and they began to dance slowly beneath the swirling snow. Diana turned to Steve and asked, "Is this what people do when there are no wars to fight?"

"This and other things," said Steve.

"What things?"

Steve shrugged and said, "I don't know. They . . . they make breakfast."

"What else?"

"Read the newspaper," said Steve. "Go to work. They . . . get married. Maybe have babies, grow old together."

Diana pondered for a moment and then asked, "What is it like?"

"No idea," admitted Steve.

"Maybe . . . once this war ends, there will be time to learn about . . . all kinds of things," Diana said.

Steve leaned closer to her and said wistfully, "I hope you're right."

The next day, Diana and her companions began to journey down the muddy road outside Veld. The grateful villagers had given them five horses. Steve was now wearing a German officer's uniform, which caused Charlie and Sammy to occasionally snicker.

"Guys, I'm fully aware that I said this job was only two days—" began Steve.

"You would get lost without us," interrupted Chief.

"Yeah, we know *Diana* is capable of looking after herself, but I'm worried *you* wouldn't make it," added Sammy.

Steve frowned and said, "There's no more money, boys."

"We've been paid enough," said Sammy.

Charlie appeared to be hesitating, so Diana rode over close to him.

"If you're coming, Charlie, perhaps you'll tell us another joke. Remind us what we're fighting for."

"Oh no!" said Sammy. "Don't *encourage* him!"

"Laughter is the best medicine," Diana continued.

A smile filled Charlie's face and he began to tell a joke. The other men groaned as they continued to travel down the road.

After a few miles, Charlie and Sammy approached Steve. Diana was riding far ahead of them.

"So, Steve," said Charlie. "You're saying that she's a real-life *Amazon*?"

"And there's a whole *island* of women like her?" asked Sammy. "And not a single man among them? How do we get there?"

"Sorry, boys," said Steve. "You're not their type."

"It's crazy," argued Charlie. "It *can't* be true."

"You saw what she did out there," said Sammy.

"The way she charged that nest of machine guns. The way she took out that tower. Maybe it's true!"

Charlie turned to Sammy and said, "You don't *really* believe all this rubbish, do you?"

After a few miles, the five companions drew closer to a giant chateau at the edge of a forest. They moved their horses off the road and took cover behind the trees. Steve stared through a pair of field glasses.

"There are dozens of German guards stationed outside the chateau," he said. "This must be the German High Command."

Steve shifted his field glasses to view a long line of limousines arriving at the front of the chateau.

"And those must be the guests for the gala," said Steve. "How in the world are we going to get in?"

"The way in is through the gate," said Chief.

"Thank you, Chief, for that ancient tribal wisdom," Charlie said sarcastically. "That's *very* helpful."

Chief sighed and climbed down from his horse. He handed the reins to Sammy and wandered deeper into the forest.

Charlie peered through the scope of his rifle and said, "If you could get through the gate, I only see one guard at the door to distract."

"It won't look at all suspicious when I come sauntering out of the woods on foot—" began Steve.

"*I* could get in," said Diana quickly.

Steve frowned and said, "You're not going in. It's too—"

"Dangerous?" challenged Diana.

"I know *how* to do stealth," said Steve. "I've been doing it my whole life. I'll follow them to wherever they're working on Maru's poison gas. Or better yet, find out where it is. Plus, we can't make a scene."

"I can be stealthy," argued Diana.

"Diana, what you're wearing doesn't exactly qualify as *undercover*," said Steve, as he pointed to her Amazon armor. "There's no way to get you in. Let me scout it out and report back. Worst case, we follow Ludendorff when he leaves, and you can use that magic lasso of yours to get him to tell us where the gas is. You have to trust me, Diana."

Suddenly, a gleaming yellow Rolls-Royce rolled into the forest. Chief was sitting behind the steering wheel.

"Where did *that* come from?" asked Steve.

Chief pointed behind him and said, "Field over there is full of them."

Sammy started jumping up and down with excitement and said, "Ooooh! Can I drive it? *Please*, let me drive it. I'll be your chauffeur!"

Steve nodded at Sammy and climbed into the backseat of the car. Sammy happily jumped into the driver's seat.

Steve leaned out the window and said, "Diana. *Please*, stay put!"

The car pulled out onto the road and headed toward the chateau.

Charlie turned to his companions and said, "We should scout the area. In case we need to beat a hasty retreat. What do you think, Diana?"

He turned around. Diana was gone.

"Uh-oh," said Charlie.

The Rolls-Royce joined the other cars lining up outside the chateau and slowly moved toward the checkpoint gate at the entrance. Sammy turned to Steve with a nervous look on his face.

"We're in trouble, Steve," he said. "The guests have invitations."

Locked in by the other cars, though, Sammy had no choice but to drive up to the entrance. A German guard reached out, waiting for Sammy to hand over an invitation.

Thinking fast, Sammy reached out both of his hands and grabbed the guard's hand.

"*Dhanyavaaad*, sahib," Sammy greeted the guard warmly. "The colonel and I wish many blessings and all manner of other things to fall upon your head."

The surprised guard pulled his hand free and turned to look at Steve in the backseat of the car. Steve leaned forward to angrily yell at Sammy.

"And *your* head is empty!" said Steve. "He wants my *invitation*, you idiot!"

Sammy lowered his eyes in shame and said, "I must apologize a *thousand* times, my masters, for my most horrid, wretched, and unworthy soul has *lost* the colonel's invitation!"

"We drive hours through this mud and filth!" Steve fumed. "You're a disgrace!"

"I am a snail," agreed Sammy. "No, a *bug*! No, the *dung* of a bug . . ."

The bewildered German guard, looking back and forth at the two men, raised his hand to wave them forward. As they pulled forward, Sammy glanced in the rearview mirror and grinned at Steve.

"Blessings be upon us," he whispered.

At the front of the chateau, Sammy opened the car door for Steve.

"Keep the car running, sahib," Steve said sternly. "And *no* joyriding."

As Steve entered the chateau, another figure was watching from the shadows at the edge of the building. It was Diana, and she shifted her cloak over her shoulder to conceal her Amazon armor. She studied the exterior of the chateau, looking for another entrance.

Just then, Diana heard the insistent honking of a car horn behind her. She turned around to see a young woman sitting in the backseat of a limousine. She had long blond hair and was wearing a beautiful blue gown. The woman was leaning over her driver, angrily honking the car's horn in an effort to get the line of cars in front of her to move faster.

"I am not spending the entire evening out here, you idiots," she declared. "Move your cars! I said, *move*!"

With a frustrated growl, the woman emerged from her car and marched up the driveway to the chateau. When she drew closer to the building, Diana stepped out of the shadows.

"What are *you* supposed to be?" said the surprised woman, as she viewed Diana's outfit.

When Diana didn't answer, the woman pushed past her and said, "Out of my way."

Diana put a hand on the woman's shoulder and studied her closely. Diana realized that they were almost the same height. She tightened her grip on the woman's shoulder.

"What are you doing?" said the outraged woman. "*Guards!*"

Diana delivered a quick martial-arts blow to the woman's neck. The woman instantly lost consciousness and fell to the ground.

That was actually . . . fun, Diana thought to herself, as she crouched down next to the woman and touched the fabric of the blue gown she was wearing.

FIFTEEN

Inside the chateau, Steve walked along the edges of the party, trying to avoid contact with any actual German officers. At the foot of a staircase, he saw a crowd gathered around Kaiser Wilhelm II, the emperor of Germany. At the other end of the room, Steve spotted General Ludendorff speaking with Doctor Maru. Steve edged closer, hoping to overhear their conversation.

"They are starting to ask where Von Hindenburg and the others are," whispered Maru.

Ludendorff sneered and said, "Soon it won't matter."

"But, General—" protested Maru.

"We continue as planned," insisted Ludendorff. "Now go. I have people to tend to beyond *you*."

As the general strode across the room, Steve moved closer to Doctor Maru.

"Excuse me," he said.

Maru turned around to look at Steve. She saw that he was holding two glasses and was offering one to her.

"I don't drink," she said, as she studied his face. "Have we met?"

"No, but I've been watching you," Steve said, and then quickly added, "Following your career, I mean. You're Doctor Isabel Maru. The most talented chemist in the German army. I'm a fan."

Maru smiled back at Steve.

"Perhaps you could show me what you're working on," he continued. "I hear it's extraordinary."

"And who are you?" Maru asked warmly.

"A man who would show you the appreciation a genius like yourself deserves," Steve said, as he moved closer to her. "A man who could . . ."

Steve's voice trailed off, as he noticed another

woman approaching him. The woman was wearing a beautiful blue gown, and her dark hair was pulled back behind her neck. It was Diana!

Maru followed Steve's gaze and noticed how closely he was looking at Diana. Maru frowned and backed away from Steve.

"I appreciate your interest in my work, but I am loyal to General Ludendorff," she said. "Besides, I see now your attention is elsewhere."

Steve sighed and turned around to confront Diana. To his dismay, he saw that she was talking to Ludendorff.

"Enjoying the party?" asked Ludendorff, as he leaned in closer to Diana.

"I confess, I'm not sure what we are celebrating," Diana said coldly.

"A German victory, of course," said Ludendorff, as he reached out his hand to invite her to dance. Diana reluctantly took his hand and followed him onto the dance floor.

"Victory?" asked Diana. "I heard that the German army just lost Veld. There are rumors that peace is very close."

"Peace is only an armistice in an endless war," said Ludendorff, drawing her closer to him.

"Thucydides," said Diana.

Ludendorff was impressed.

"You know your ancient Greeks," he said. "They understood that war is a god. One that requires human sacrifice. And in exchange, war gives man purpose. A chance to rise above his petty, mortal little life and be better than he is."

"Only *one* of the many gods believed in that," declared Diana, as she pulled away from Ludendorff. "And he was wrong."

"You know nothing about the gods—" began Ludendorff.

A voice interrupted him. It was a German soldier, nervously standing a few feet away.

"General?" he said.

Ludendorff bowed to Diana and said, "My apologies. You'll excuse me."

As Ludendorff walked away, Steve rushed over to Diana and grabbed her hand. He pulled her onto the dance floor and whispered angrily in her ear.

"What are you *doing*?" he demanded. "You agreed to wait."

"You agree to do things all the time and then don't do them," Diana responded, as she pulled her hand free. "Let me go!"

"You can't kill Ludendorff *inside* German High Command," said Steve, as he reached for her other hand. "I can't let you do this."

"What I do isn't up to you," Diana angrily replied.

Using just her fingertips, she pushed Steve away from her. He almost toppled to the floor.

Diana ran out of the room, searching for Ludendorff. Steve was close behind her.

When Diana emerged from the back of the chateau, she looked around, searching for Ludendorff. She saw him climbing into an armored transport vehicle. Maru and four soldiers were already inside the vehicle.

"To the airfield ... now!" commanded Ludendorff.

The vehicle sped down the road.

"Diana!" yelled Steve as he ran out of the chateau. He looked around, but there was no sign of her.

Suddenly, he heard a sound in the nearby forest. It was Diana riding her horse. Her Amazon armor glinted in the moonlight. She had ripped off her blue dress, and its tattered remnants floated to the ground behind her. She raced off in pursuit of Ludendorff.

Steve stood in the road, watching helplessly as Diana galloped after the general. He had failed in his mission, and Diana had left him behind. Ludendorff and Maru were free to launch an attack of the poison gas.

Steve pondered his options. Then he ran toward the dark forest and disappeared from sight.

SIXTEEN

A security post stood at the entrance to the German High Command airfield. The three guards in the security post barely had a chance to look up as the armored vehicle carrying Ludendorff sped past them and drove onto the airfield. The vehicle screeched to a halt in front of the airfield's control tower. Ludendorff and his companions quickly entered the base of the tower.

Five minutes later, a very different visitor arrived at the security post. It was Diana atop her galloping horse. The guards jumped to their feet to block her way, but Diana reached down with both arms and knocked the guards aside like they were bowling pins.

Diana reined in her horse and scanned the airfield. There were German soldiers marching everywhere. She looked up at the top of the control tower. There she saw Ludendorff, peering over the edge of a balcony. She turned around and saw two German soldiers, their guns drawn, running toward her.

Diana jumped off her horse and launched herself into the air. She landed on top of the two soldiers and knocked them to the ground. She then grabbed her golden lasso and started twirling it above her head. The glowing lasso soared through the air and looped around a German soldier on the balcony of the control tower. Diana gave a quick tug on the lasso and yanked the soldier down to his knees. She then climbed up her golden rope and jumped up onto the balcony.

Ludendorff had moved inside the control tower. Diana stepped forward and unsheathed her sword. When she entered the room, he turned to face her.

"Nice to see you again," he said. "This is a surprise."

With a cold smile on his face, Ludendorff pointed

a gun directly at Diana.

"But I have things to do," he said.

Diana raised her sword in her right hand and said, "I am Diana of Themyscira, daughter of Hippolyta."

Ludendorff bowed his head slightly and said, "As magnificent a creature as you are, you are no match for me."

"We'll see about that," Diana said.

Ludendorff squeezed the trigger of his gun and fired. Diana raised her left hand, blocking the bullet with her bracelet. The bullet ricocheted back toward Ludendorff's gun, causing the weapon to explode in his hand. He cried out in pain.

Diana stepped forward and raised her sword.

"I, daughter of Hippolyta, came here to complete the mission of the Amazons to end this war."

Ludendorff ran to a wall and grabbed a bayoneted rifle that was mounted there. He lunged toward Diana, using the rifle as a spear, but she was too fast for him and jumped out of the way. Her sword sliced through the air and plunged into his body.

He fell to the ground, dead.

Diana's breath was heavy. She stood for a few

moments, staring at the lifeless body. Then she heard a noise coming from the airfield. It was a German commander, screaming at his troops. Diana ran to the balcony and looked out over the airfield. Her heart dropped.

Diana saw hundreds of German soldiers marching in formation toward a large carrier aircraft. The soldiers were all wearing customized gas masks. Diana gasped, as she realized that these were the special gas masks developed by Doctor Maru to withstand her poison gas. How could one person—even a superstrong Amazon—stop so many soldiers?

Steve ran along the edge of the airfield, searching for Charlie, Sammy, and Chief. He soon found them, huddled together behind a stack of wooden crates outside an airplane hangar.

"Where's Diana?" asked Sammy.

"I don't know," said Steve. "We're on our own."

Charlie peered through the scope of his rifle, studying the gas-masked soldiers.

"I can't see where they're taking the gas," he said.

Sammy turned to stare at the edge of the airfield's runway. There he saw the soldiers loading the gas-laden bombs into the giant aircraft.

"Wherever Diana is, I think we're gonna need her," he said.

Steve motioned to his companions to follow him. Moving slowly, they edged closer to the hangar and then ran behind the building. They crept up quietly behind four German soldiers.

BLAM!

Charlie swung his rifle through the air and slammed it against the four soldiers. They fell to the ground, unconscious. Minutes later, Steve and his team emerged from behind the hangar. Their heads were covered in gas masks, and they were wearing German flight jackets. They moved with confidence toward the giant aircraft.

Sammy quickly boarded the plane and made his way to the huge stockpile of bombs that had been loaded on board. He peered closely at the bombs. These small mechanical devices with intricate wiring could cause so much destruction.

Chief walked slowly toward a group of German

soldiers that were huddled around a map. Without speaking, he moved closer to the soldiers, craning his head to look at the map. He gasped silently when he saw the target location for the plane. It was London!

Steve walked to the front of the plane, where he found an open toolbox. He grabbed a crowbar from the box and looked around to make sure no one was watching. Then he wedged the crowbar into a small metal panel on the side of the plane, hoping he might be able to sabotage the wiring.

"Hey! You!" a voice called out.

Steve spun around to see a German soldier approaching him. The soldier lifted his rifle.

THUMP!

Charlie swung his rifle butt against the soldier's head, knocking him to the ground.

Steve smiled with gratitude, but his smile quickly faded when he looked over Charlie's shoulder. Doctor Maru and three soldiers were walking toward the plane. Steve quickly pulled Charlie out of the way, and the two men faded into the shadows. They then ran to the back wall of the hangar, where they found Chief and Sammy.

"The plane! It's going to London," said Chief.

"What if we radio ahead?" suggested Charlie. "They could shoot it down."

"If it crashes, it wipes out everyone around," said Steve. "We have to ground it."

"If it accidentally crashes, same thing here," argued Sammy. "It'll kill everyone over fifty square miles."

Steve looked out at the airfield. Doctor Maru was standing in front of the plane. The three German soldiers were climbing on board.

"Go! Go now!" commanded Doctor Maru. She then turned swiftly on her heel and marched back toward the hangar.

Steve frowned and said, "The pilot, the copilot, and the bombardier . . . they're getting on the plane."

A truck parked in front of the plane started to pull the giant craft away from the hangar. The plane was moving slowly toward the runway.

Charlie crouched down and pointed his rifle at the truck. His years on the battlefield had led him to this moment. This was the most important bullet of his life. He squeezed the trigger and fired directly into the truck's engine. Sparks and smoke filled the air, as the truck shuddered to a stop, halting the plane behind it.

Steve jumped to his feet and started running toward the entrance to the hangar.

"The lab!" he called out. "Maru's lab . . . it's inside the hangar. Let's go!"

His three companions exchanged looks.

"If we go in there, we're not coming back," said Sammy.

Chief and Charlie shrugged. Then the three men ran after Steve.

Gunshots rang out as soon as Steve and his teammates stepped into the hangar. Doctor Maru was standing near a lab table. She was frantically gathering notebooks and papers in her hands. Next to her were large metal drums filled with chemicals.

As Charlie fired at the German soldiers, Steve and Chief ran into the hangar and started knocking over the lab equipment. Sammy was close behind, setting explosive charges on top of the metal drums.

"Let's go!" yelled Steve, as he and his team ran from the building. As soon as they emerged, Steve and Chief wheeled around and tossed two grenades into the hangar. Then all four men hit the ground.

KER-BLAM!

A giant explosion detonated behind them, sending a huge ball of fire into the air. Black smoke filled the air as the hangar burst into flames.

Steve and his team had only seconds to savor their victory. Dozens of German soldiers began to fire at them. The soldiers surrounded the four men on every side. Charlie continued to fire his rifle over and over.

Suddenly, when Charlie squeezed the trigger, nothing happened. His face fell as he realized that he was out of bullets.

"Uh-oh," he said to his friends. "Looks like this might be the end."

SEVENTEEN

The four men huddled close to each other, watching as the German soldiers slowly advanced on them.

Just then, a bright bolt of lightning struck the airfield. The German soldiers spun around and then fell back in confusion. The soldiers watched with astonishment as a single figure started running down the airfield, moving toward them. It was a woman.

A bright aura of energy surrounded Diana as she ran toward the soldiers. With a cry of anger, she swung her shield through the air and crashed into the soldiers. One after another, the soldiers fell to the ground, knocked unconscious.

Minutes later, Diana stood triumphant on the airfield. She turned to look at Steve and his friends. With disbelieving looks on their faces, the four men slowly climbed to their feet and moved toward her.

The sound of an engine filled the air. Steve turned around and saw a giant tank moving across the airfield. It was heading straight toward Diana.

"Diana," he called. "Look out!"

Diana spun around to face the tank. She planted her feet firmly on the ground and reached out both arms. Just as the tank was about to collide into Diana, she grabbed the front of the tank and lifted it off the ground. As she held the giant vehicle above her, a German soldier—the tank's driver—tumbled out of the tank and landed on the ground in front of Diana.

The young soldier's eyes were closed, and he groaned softly. He then opened his eyes to discover Diana standing above him and holding the giant tank aloft.

"Please, no . . . ," the young soldier pleaded, as he

raised his hands to protect himself.

Diana looked down at the soldier. It would be so easy to crush him. Diana's anger grew, thinking about Maru's poison gas and this soldier's intent to carry out her evil plan. Diana thought back to what her mother had told her: *Mankind is easily corruptible.*

They do not deserve you.

Diana closed her eyes. Her thoughts suddenly were filled with images of Steve and his teammates. She thought of the sacrifices that they had made. The bravery they had shown.

Quietly, to herself, Diana said, "No. The gods made us, the Amazons, to influence men's hearts with love and to restore peace to the world."

A golden glow began to surround Diana as she opened her eyes. As she placed the tank back on the ground, a light rain began to fall.

Soon, the rain washed away the black smoke from the sky. A golden dawn broke through the clouds. In the distance, Diana could hear the sound of people cheering in a nearby village. The last bits of smoke drifted away as the sun rose. A ray of sunlight lit her face.

She watched as Steve and his friends tended to the wounds of the German soldiers. A smile filled her face.

"I wanted to protect the world," she said to herself. "To end war and bring peace to mankind. But now I know . . ."

She paused to collect her thoughts.

"I've touched the darkness that lives in between the light. Seen the worst of this world, and the best. Seen the terrible things that men do to each other in the name of hatred . . . and the lengths they will go to for love."

As she walked over to join her friends, she said softly, "Love always beating its way through the mire. Love refusing to be anything but true and pure. Because of love, I will never be the same."

She crouched down to wrap a cloth bandage around a German soldier's head wound.

The first part of Diana's journey was over. Now she would begin the journey to become the hero the world needed.

She was ready to become Wonder Woman.